MISSION TO MALGOR

THE JUNIOR NOVEL

Adapted by Lauren Alexander
Based on the original screenplay by Kirk De Micco

PSS!
PRICE STERN SLOAN

PRICE STERN SLOAN
Published by the Penguin Group
Penguin Group (USA) Inc., 375 Hudson Street, New York, New York 10014, USA
Penguin Group (Canada), 90 Eglinton Avenue East, Suite 700, Toronto, Ontario M4P 2Y3, Canada
(a division of Pearson Penguin Canada Inc.)
Penguin Books Ltd., 80 Strand, London WC2R 0RL, England
Penguin Group Ireland, 25 St. Stephen's Green, Dublin 2, Ireland
(a division of Penguin Books Ltd.)
Penguin Group (Australia), 250 Camberwell Road, Camberwell, Victoria 3124, Australia
(a division of Pearson Australia Group Pty. Ltd.)
Penguin Books India Pvt. Ltd., 11 Community Centre, Panchsheel Park,
New Delhi—110 017, India
Penguin Group (NZ), 67 Apollo Drive, Rosedale, North Shore 0632, New Zealand
(a division of Pearson New Zealand Ltd.)
Penguin Books (South Africa) (Pty.) Ltd., 24 Sturdee Avenue,
Rosebank, Johannesburg 2196, South Africa

Penguin Books Ltd., Registered Offices: 80 Strand, London WC2R 0RL, England

PRICE STERN SLOAN

Space Chimps TM & © 2008 Vanguard Animation, LLC. All Rights Reserved.
Published by Price Stern Sloan, a division of Penguin Young Readers Group,
345 Hudson Street, New York, New York 10014.
PSS! is a registered trademark of Penguin Group (USA) Inc. Printed in the U.S.A.

Library of Congress Control Number: 2007049056

ISBN 978-0-8431-3268-7   10 9 8 7 6 5 4 3 2 1

CHAPTER ONE

Ten, nine, eight, seven, six, five, four, three, two, one . . . Blast off!

A rocket shot into space, leaving a fiery tail in its wake. The astronaut inside was ready to explore the unknown reaches of space. But wait! That wasn't a human astronaut inside—it was a chimp named Ham I!

Ham I was the first American to boldly go where no man, or chimp, had ever gone before. He was a national hero—an international superstar.

Years after Ham I's historic space trip, his grandson, Ham III, decided to follow in his grandfather's footsteps. Ham III loved flying through space—just not outer space. Ham worked at a circus, and he was about to be shot out of a cannon.

"Ladies and gentlemen," the ringmaster called out. "Strap yourselves in as we embark on a mission to the stars."

Hearing this, Ham said, "Space, stars, blah, blah, blah. Enough with the lecture, let's get to the action."

An old chimp named Houston waddled up to Ham. "Aim high, buckle up," he said.

"And chin down, opposable thumbs in," Ham added. "When are you going to stop worrying about me, Houston? Space is in my veins."

Houston smiled. "And between your ears," he said, placing a helmet on Ham's head.

"It's showtime!" Ham shouted.

Ham looked around the colorful circus tent. People of all ages were sitting in the stands.

Some were eating cotton candy, and others were munching on popcorn and peanuts. He saw kids waving circus banners and spinning lights. But no matter what they were doing, they were all there to see him.

The ringmaster took a deep breath. "Here we go," he said to the crowd. "Let's make some noise. Let's tear the roof off this tent. We're gonna go bananas!"

Hearing his cue, Ham raised his thumb and jumped into the cannon. "Prepare to be amazified!" he shouted.

Using his foot, Houston struck a match and lit the cannon's fuse.

"Say it with me!" the ringmaster addressed the crowd. "T-minus three! Two! One! Blast off!"

Kaboom!

Ham shot out of the cannon and flew out into the night sky through a hole in the tent top.

"Yeeahoo!" Ham shouted as he rocketed through the air. He loved the thrill of flying. His heart pounded as he headed into the stratosphere. He was so high above the Earth that he felt as though he could almost touch outer space. Higher and higher he flew. He felt so happy, so weightless.

Suddenly, he started to fall. *Stall and burn*, Ham thought, feeling deflated. He looked down toward Earth at his target—a red and white bull's-eye painted on the top of the circus tent.

"Mission control has just sighted Ham," the ringmaster told the crowd. "Keep your eyes on the landing pad."

Houston drove a flatbed truck filled with hay bales into the ring so Ham would have something soft to land on. He parked the truck on a mark on the floor, directly under the hole in the tent. Houston looked up and saw Ham coming in fast.

"No monkey business. Stay on target, hotshot," Houston muttered to himself.

"The big finale's coming up!" Ham shouted as he careened back to Earth, his cape flapping over his head.

Ham knew he should stay on course, but he just couldn't resist having some fun. He started to flip and spin in the air as he came in for his landing. Flip, fall, spin, fall, twirl, fall . . . *crash!*

Ham ripped though the wrong part of the tent. Instead of landing on the bull's-eye target, he crash-landed on top of the one-man band. The musician, who was a seal, flailed his flippers in anger.

"He's always showboating," Houston said, shaking his head.

The crowd was on its feet. Was Ham okay? Was this the end of the flying chimp?

Seeing the crowd's concern, the ringmaster stepped up to the microphone. "It's all good, folks," he said, clearing his voice. "That's why he wears a helmet."

Ham looked up, dazed, and shot a thumbs-up to his fans.

High above the circus, something bright streaked across the sky. It was the *Infinity* probe, and it had just been launched into outer space. It soared up past the moon and stars. Suddenly, it was pulled toward a spinning vortex of energy and light—it was a wormhole. Then, *whoosh*, it was sucked into the wormhole and pushed into another galaxy very, very faraway from Earth.

One of the planets in this other galaxy was named Malgor. On Malgor's surface, a little blue alien child was watching the sky. "Look!" he shouted. "A flutter-eye!"

He ran through the town chasing the flutter-eye,

and soon a group of alien children was following him. They all wanted to see where the flutter-eye would land.

The children chased the flutter-eye to the outskirts of the town, where the volcano loomed over the village. Silver freznar bubbled up from the volcano and pooled around its base. Only one person lived in this part of town. His creepy ramshackle hut stood right on the edge of a deep pool of freznar. The kids watched as the flying creature flew toward the front door of the hut. Too frightened to get any closer, they stopped in their tracks.

Slam! The front door of the hut flew open and a hulking blue figure stood in the doorway. "Can't you brats read?" he shouted.

"Zartog!" the children cried in frightened tones.

"Keep away from my house!" Zartog said,

pointing to a sign that was hanging outside his doorway.

"Ha! We can't wait until the volcano explodes on Triple Sunday and freezes you and your stupid hut," a brave kid spoke up. The silvery freznar that came out of the volcano froze anyone who touched it.

Just then, Zartog noticed the flutter-eye and slammed his door on it. *Squish!* He peeled the flutter-eye off the wall and dipped it into the pool of freznar that was next to his house. When he pulled the flutter-eye out, it was frozen like a statue!

"You monster!" a child shouted. "Why did you freeze that poor flutter-eye? It didn't do anything to you!"

Zartog let out an evil laugh. "If I could catch you punks, I'd dunk you in the freznar, too!"

"No wonder everyone in the town hates you," another child said.

"Just the way I like it!" Zartog replied. "I wouldn't want to live like *you*, with your colorful houses and stupid smiles."

Just then, a loud *whoosh* filled the air. Everyone looked up. The *Infinity* probe was about to land, and it was headed straight toward Zartog!

"Craplar!" Zartog shouted as he tried to run.

But there was no time. The *Infinity* was falling too fast. In a second, Zartog would be history!

CHAPTER TWO

The *Infinity* whizzed through the sky and crashed directly into Zartog's hut. The hut collapsed into a pile of rubble right on top of Zartog.

But under the debris, Zartog was still alive. He rubbed his eyes and pulled himself out of the wreckage. Suddenly, something shiny caught his eye. He cleared the remains of his hut away and found himself face-to-face with the *Infinity* probe. Suddenly, a robotic arm shot out of the probe and grabbed him! The children screamed and ran.

"I am the *Infinity* probe from the planet Earth," the probe said. "Please lie back and enjoy a brief introduction to Earth as I perform a full-body examination for purely scientific purposes. Presentation beginning now!"

A screen flipped down and images flashed before Zartog's eyes. "Since the dawn of time, man has made some incredible achievements in culture and civilization. He's created wonders in architecture, art, and music." Pictures of beautiful buildings and statues flashed across the screen while soothing music played.

Then, the images switched abruptly to dancing girls, a rock band, and sleek sports cars. Zartog smiled. He liked what he saw. These people knew how to have fun!

"I'm going to live like them," Zartog said, pushing a button on the screen's control panel. The *Infinity* prover emerged from inside of the probe. It had wheels and long robotic arms.

Zartog smiled a greedy smile. He knew just what to do with the prover. "A new day has come, and that day is Zartog!" he shouted as he hopped onto the prover.

Pressing some buttons, Zartog and the prover lurched forward. "Aaah!" Zartog screamed as the prover careened out of control.

"Aaah!" the children screamed, running away from Zartog and the prover.

Back on Earth, a group of schoolchildren were taking a tour of the Space Agency. Their noses were pressed up against a glass window as they looked at three chimpanzees.

"The Simian Space Program was started in the 1960s. And these chimpanzees are just like the ones used in the first space mission," their tour guide, Dr. Smothers, explained.

"When do they go into space?" one of the students wanted to know.

"They don't," Dr. Smothers answered. "They're

just exhibits of the history of the Space Agency."

Just then, the senator pushed through the doors and strode past Dr. Smothers. He didn't even bother to say hello. Something was definitely wrong. The senator provided funding for the space program, so if he was in a bad mood the space program could be in trouble.

Dr. Smothers was right. The senator started yelling as soon as he entered the mission-control room.

"What do you mean *lost*?" the senator shouted at the three scientists who were working in the room.

"Senator, the *Infinity* was drawn off course by a magnetic attraction from a dimensional anomaly in the space-time continuum," Dr. Jagu explained.

The senator heaved a big sigh. "In *English*," he said.

"It was sucked into a wormhole," Dr. Jagu said.

"My constituents care about potholes, not

wormholes," the senator said angrily. "Do you know how many potholes we can fix for five billion dollars?"

The scientists didn't know what to say. They knew that it cost a lot of money to send the *Infinity* to space. And they knew that now that the *Infinity* was lost, all of that money was lost, too. They had to figure out a way to get the *Infinity* back.

"As you can see from this image, the *Infinity* has landed on a planet in a crater filled with H_2O," Dr. Jagu explained.

"That means water," Dr. Bob put in.

The senator stamped his foot. "I know what that means!" he shouted.

The scientists tried to remain calm, but the senator looked like he was about to explode with anger.

Finally Dr. Poole broke the silence. "You know, if there is water where the *Infinity* landed, there is a good chance that some form of life exists there also. Maybe we could send a mission to explore the planet and retrieve the probe."

The senator's eyes grew wide. What a great idea! "I want astronauts over there, pronto," he told the scientists. "Finding aliens would certainly impress my voters!"

"We can't send astronauts!" Dr. Bob exclaimed. "We have no idea what sending humans through a wormhole would do to them. It could kill them all, and that would not impress your voters."

The scientists and the senator continued to argue. But what they didn't know was that the three chimps behind the glass in the Space Agency were listening to their conversation. And they were excited! This was the chance they had been waiting for!

Quickly, Comet, one of the chimps, began typing on his computer. With the press of a button, he sent a photo of himself and the other Space Chimps to the scientists.

Seconds later, the photo popped up on Dr. Bob's computer screen. It gave Dr. Bob an idea. "We could send the chimps," he said, looking at the photo.

"Chimps?" the senator asked incredulously. Then he thought about it for a moment. "Chimps, not humans? It's better than nothing," he said, scratching his chin. "Show me what you got."

"Guys! We got a mission!" Comet shouted to the other chimps, Luna and Titan.

Dr. Smothers led the senator to the window of the Simian Center. "Titan, Luna, and Comet are fully prepared for the mission," she explained, motioning toward the chimps. "They've been training for this their whole lives."

The senator took one look at the well-behaved chimps and said, "Training, schmaining! These chimps are boring. They're chimp nerds! What this mission needs is some PR—some sizzle to grab the media's attention. It needs a chimp with the right stuff. Someone like him." He pointed to a photo of Ham I that hung inside the chimps' room.

But Ham I was long gone. There would never be another chimp like him. Or would there?

CHAPTER THREE

Ham drove a car wildly around the circus tent, steering with his feet. As he drove, he juggled sticks of dynamite with his hands.

"Ladies and gentlemen," the ringmaster called out. "Do not try this at home."

Just then, Ham pulled out a blowtorch from under his seat. "Big finale coming right up," he said as he lit the dynamite.

Houston couldn't believe his ears. "No, no, no!" he hissed at Ham from the edge of the tent. "That *was* the finale. What do you mean it's coming up? Stay focused!"

Ham shook his head and sighed. "Quit worrying,

Houston. They're going to love this one."

Ham continued to drive around the ring, now steering with his hands and juggling with his feet. The crowd cheered. Ham was putting on an amazing show!

Suddenly, Ham lost control. He gripped the steering wheel harder, but it was no use. He crashed right into the one-seal band, again. Then the dynamite shot through the air and hit Ham right in the head. *Boom!* The crowd gasped.

"Not to worry, folks," the ringmaster told the crowd. "It's all part of the act."

As the smoke cleared, the crowd could see that Ham was okay, if a little singed. Ham tried to give his signature thumbs-up, but his thumb was injured. Houston helped Ham up and rushed him back to his trailer as the crowd left the circus.

"Quit fidgeting, Ham," Houston said as he bandaged Ham's thumb. "I promised your grandpa I'd look after you. You have to stop this showboating."

Just then, the trailer door burst open. The ringmaster was standing in front of the doorway, trying to keep a woman from coming inside. "You can't take him!" the ringmaster shouted.

Ham and Houston looked at the two humans. What were they talking about? Who was going to take whom?

The woman looked at Houston. "Wow, he's older than I expected."

Houston was offended. "Well, you are no spring chicken, either."

Then the woman set her eyes upon Ham. "He's so cute!" she exclaimed.

"I'm such eye candy," Ham said, smoothing back his fur at the compliment.

"I'm Dr. Smothers," the lady said. "And you are going into space—just like your grandfather."

Ham could not believe his ears. "Space?" He shook his head. "Wrong answer. Not my thing. The only space for me is MySpace." He jumped up and pushed Dr. Smothers toward the door.

But Dr. Smothers did not realize that Ham was trying to get rid of her. "Well, he seems very excited to go," she said as she left the trailer.

"Kid, this is a chance for you to really make something of yourself—to follow in your grandfather's footsteps," Houston told Ham.

Ham shook his head. "I'm the star of *my* show," he told Houston. "Why would I want to be the warm-up act for some human astronaut?"

Houston couldn't understand Ham's attitude. Ham's grandfather was a real astronaut. He was famous—his face had been on the covers of newspapers and magazines. He even got to meet the president! If Ham agreed to go on this space mission, he could have what his grandfather had and more.

Suddenly, the trailer began to shake. Ham ran to the window to see what was happening. His trailer was being lifted off the ground by a sky-crane helicopter! It looked like Ham was going to the Space Agency whether he liked it or not.

"Er, Houston," Ham said. "We have a problem!"

Inside the Simian Center, Luna, Titan, and Comet were anxiously awaiting Ham's arrival.

"Here he comes!" Luna shouted.

The chimps lined up and stood proudly at attention.

Ham and Houston were shoved into the room, and the door was closed behind them. "I know my rights! I'm calling the ASPCA!" Ham screamed.

The other chimps' jaws dropped. *This* was Ham?

Titan sucked in his stomach and saluted.

"Commander Titan," he introduced himself.

Ham stared at the chimp.

Luna stepped forward. "Lieutenant Luna. It's an honor, sir," she said with a salute.

Ham smiled. "Aren't you a bit all right? Luna means moon in Latin," he said.

Luna was impressed. "That's right, sir."

"Why don't we skip out back and take a little trip to the moona, huh, Luna?" Ham said.

Luna couldn't believe her ears. Ham was supposed to be an astronaut. Why was he flirting with her?

Next, Comet tried to introduce himself. "Name's Comet. Computers and electronics. I look forward to serving you."

Ham shook his head. "Sorry, kid, but I'm not sticking around." He pointed toward the door. "Let's go, Houston."

"Sir, with all due respect," Luna said, trying to

prevent Ham from leaving, "you've been selected for a *mission* of historical significance in the noble pursuit of . . ."

"Land of the free, home of the brave, yada, yada, yada," Ham said, cutting her off. "Listen, the only mission I have is to entertain. Watch and learn."

Ham showed the chimps his empty hands. Then magically, ping-pong balls appeared. He twirled them between his fingers. Then, just as suddenly as the balls appeared, they disappeared. And just when the chimps thought he was done, the balls appeared again.

"Abracadabble," Ham said.

"Cool!" Comet exclaimed.

"Perfect," Titan said, rolling his eyes. "He's a joke."

Just then, Ham spotted something hanging on the wall. "What are those?" he asked.

"Rocket packs," Luna answered. "We're demonstrating them to the press on Saturday."

Ham's eyes grew wide. Looking at the rocket packs, he knew exactly how he would bust out of the Space Center.

CHAPTER FOUR

On Planet Malgor, Zartog was riding through town on the prover. An evil smile lit up his hideous face.

"Quake with fear! Lord Zartog is here!" he shouted as he knocked down one alien house after another.

The aliens ran for their lives. But the faster they ran, the faster Zartog drove. Soon Zartog was herding them all straight toward the volcano!

"By now you are all aware of the insane power I command with my big shiny what-a-ma-thingy," Zartog announced. "Are there any among you who oppose my rule?"

One alien raised his hand. "Why are you in charge? Just because some stupid sky beast fell on your hut?"

Hearing this, Zartog became irate. How dare this alien question his rule! In one swift move, Zartog snatched the alien with the prover's claw and dunked him in the freznar. When Zartog pulled the alien out of the liquid, he was frozen solid. The alien was still alive, but he was frozen inside the shell of freznar. Zartog was satisfied with his work. "See what happens to those who oppose me?" Zartog shouted at the masses before him.

The volcano rumbled above them. Zartog looked up at the sky. The three suns were closer together now, and he knew that Triple Sunday was almost here. It was time to get to work . . .

At the training center, the chimps were busy preparing for their mission. Ham, Titan, and

Luna were strapped into a centrifuge machine. The centrifuge machine would spin them around very quickly—just like what would happen inside the wormhole. As the machine spun, Ham turned to look at Luna. The machine was spinning so fast that her face looked as if it were being pulled back. It looked like she was smiling.

"Smile if you think I'm cute," Ham said teasingly.

Titan growled. He did not like that Ham was fooling around. Training was serious business!

When the machine finally stopped spinning, Comet wanted to get on.

"Ah, poor little Comet thinks he's going into space," Dr. Smothers said, shaking her head. "Too bad there's only room for three chimps in the ship." She and the other scientists knew that only Luna, Titan, and Ham were going on the mission.

Comet hung his head. He was crushed. He'd been training for a mission his entire life.

"We'll need you here," Luna said, putting her arm around Comet. "You'll be our eyes and ears."

Comet knew Luna was right. They'd need someone to stay down on Earth to look after them. And with his computer skills, Comet was just the chimp for the job—no one could do it as well as he could!

For the rest of the day, the chimps trained for their mission. They all took the work seriously—except for Ham. He monkeyed around on the treadmill and didn't even try to learn the correct buttons to press on the spaceship's control panel.

Houston was furious at Ham. "When are you going to straighten up and fly right?" he asked.

Ham looked mischievously at the rocket packs. "Saturday, at about ten o'clock," he answered.

Just then, Comet came running up to Ham. "I made these banana phones for the mission. I think they might work through the wormhole."

"You made these?" Ham asked looking at the phones.

Comet told Ham that he only modified them—he changed some things here and there to make the phones better. But Ham wasn't impressed. He didn't think he'd have a need for the phone. After all, he was going to make his big escape before the mission took off, right?

On Saturday morning, the senator stood in the middle of the rocket garden, addressing a crowd. Surrounding him were the historic *Apollo* rockets and a space shuttle prototype.

"My fellow citizens, we stand on the verge of history," the senator said. "The rocket we are going to launch will travel across the cosmos to a distant planet, where we hope to finally answer the age-old question, 'Is there intelligent life out there?'"

A murmur arose from the crowd.

"It's a dangerous mission, but luckily, we have just the astronauts for the job—the Space Chimps," the senator continued.

Titan, Luna, and Ham were led out onto the stage by the scientists. The chimps were dressed in their space gear, with rocket packs strapped to their backs.

The crowd cheered. Cameras flashed. Reporters furiously scribbled down notes. This was a historic moment.

"Ham I was the first chimp to boldly go where no American had gone before, and now his grandson is going to follow in his footsteps. And here he is, a symbol of our country's once and future greatness, Ham the Third!" the senator announced.

"To infinity and a blonde!" Ham exclaimed. And with that, he pressed a button on his rocket pack and blasted straight up into the air.

Up! Up! Up! *Thunk!* Ham zoomed right into the

bottom of a news helicopter. The crowd winced. Dazed, Ham flew around wildly.

"Left thumb stop, up, down," Ham said, fumbling with the controls. But he couldn't get the rocket back under control. He took a nosedive toward the crowd. Everyone ducked.

"I'm on TV!" Ham shouted dizzily. Then, he crashed smack into a rocket in the park. The rocket fell forward, hitting another rocket, which hit another rocket, which hit another rocket—it was like watching dominos fall. The people in the crowd ran for their lives. Soon every rocket in the park had fallen, and the crowd was gone. Ham lay unconscious at the senator's feet.

The senator looked at Ham and scowled. This was not what he had planned for the day.

CHAPTER FIVE

"T-minus ten, nine, eight, seven . . ." a technician said.

Ham thought he was dreaming. Slowly, he opened his eyes and looked around. He was sitting inside of a spaceship with Luna and Titan. "What kind of simulator is this? It looks really realistic," he asked.

Luna shot him a look. "That's because it is," she said.

". . . two, one. Liftoff!" the tech announced.

Gravity pushed Ham back into his seat as the rocket launched. He looked out the porthole next to him. "Guys, this isn't a simulation, is it?"

Luna shook her head. "We are now officially Space Chimps!"

Ham's stomach sunk. This was it—the real deal. There was no escaping now.

Luna and Titan got to work. They had trained hard, and they were ready to make this mission a success. Luna picked up her space manual to review some procedures.

"Oh, stewardess," Ham called out to Luna. "Can you get me a pillow and a blanket?"

Luna ignored him.

Ham unbuckled his seat belt and floated over to a bunch of bananas. "Look! No hands! No feet! No butt!" he said, juggling the bananas.

"Stay in your seat. Juggling our food is against regulations!" Luna yelled at him.

Ham didn't listen. He kept on juggling and flipping in the zero gravity. He was having a ball!

"Back on Earth, your insubordinate behavior

would get you chimp-martialed!" Titan added, getting out of his seat and floating toward Ham.

"Commander, violence is against the Primate Directive," Luna cautioned Titan.

Titan knew she was right. Even though Ham was making his blood boil, he could not physically harm him. Titan went back to reviewing the landing process.

Luna also went back to work. "Engaging 3-D matrix," she said.

Ham pretended to do work. He pressed a button on the control panel. "Fire photon torpedoes!" he said. Oxygen masks fell from the ceiling.

Titan had had enough of Ham's crazy antics. "You're a threat to the mission!" he shouted.

Titan jumped out of his seat and lunged at Ham. But Ham was too quick. He dodged Titan's outstretched arm in one swift move.

Titan wasn't about to give up, though. He

bounced around the cabin, trying to nab Ham.

Luna tried to ignore what was happening. "Orbital stabilizers, check. Auxiliary thrusters, check. Collision detector . . ."

"Windshield-wiper fluid, check!" Ham joked.

"Gotcha!" Titan said, grabbing Ham's arm. "I can't take this for another seventy-three million light-years."

"Ow!" Ham cried. "Easy on the fur, furious George."

"Unruly crew member has been detained. Enact regulation number 815," Titan said.

"What's that?" Ham wanted to know.

His question was quickly answered as he found himself tethered to the outside of the ship.

"Guys, I have to pee!" Ham called to the others inside.

When no one answered him, Ham pulled himself back to the air lock and jimmied the door open. Then he tiptoed through the cabin to the bathroom, making sure not to disturb Luna and Titan. When Ham flushed the toilet, the roll of toilet paper got sucked out into space.

"Oops!" Ham said, watching as the toilet paper floated toward the wormhole.

On the other side of the wormhole, Zartog was sitting on the prover, observing his alien slaves at work.

"That's not straight enough," he growled at a slave who was laying bricks.

"And that's too straight," he barked at the next slave down the line.

"I'll fix it right away, sir," the slave answered, but Zartog wasn't listening. He was studying the construction in the distance.

"Splork!" Zartog shouted.

"Yes, Lord Zartog," Splork quickly replied as

he hurried over to stand at Zartog's side.

"Have your men fixed the carnacs?"

"Yes, Lord Zartog," Splork said.

"Perfect," Zartog said with a satisfied grin. "Soon the house of Zartog will be finished. It's going to be magnificent!"

"It's a shame the volcano will destroy it when the three suns line up on Triple Sunday," Splork said humbly.

Zartog looked up in the sky. Sure enough, the three suns were drawing closer together. But instead of looking scared, Zartog looked happy. He had a plan. He had had the aliens build a system of pipes. When the volcano erupted, the freznar would travel through the pipes, away from his palace. His palace would be safe, but the rest of the village would be frozen.

Zartog chuckled to himself. His plan was genius!

The ship accelerated as it got closer and closer to the wormhole.

"Approaching dimensional anomaly entry," Luna said.

The ship began to shake and the lights inside the cabin dimmed.

"Brace for event threshold," Titan announced.

The cabin shook even more violently. Luna, Titan, and Ham were pinned back in their seats, trying desperately to fight the increasing gravitational force.

"Approaching five g's, six g's, eight g's," Luna said, fighting to stay awake under the immense pressure.

But the force of gravity was too strong. Luna and Titan passed out.

"Hey, guys! This is no time for a power nap!" Ham said, trying to shake the other chimps awake.

It was no use. Luna and Titan were out cold. Unable to resist, Ham picked up a Sharpie marker and drew a funny face on Titan's helmet. Just then the cabin was flooded with light. The ship was entering the wormhole.

Frantically, Ham started pressing buttons on the control panel. "Welcome to InStar," a female voice said. "How can I help you?"

But Ham had no time to ask for help. The ship was rushing through the wormhole. As he looked out the window, Ham spotted a planet. At first he was relieved, but then he realized that they were headed straight toward it. In another minute they would crash!

Ham tried to shake Luna and Titan awake again. "Wake up! Wake up! You've got to land this thing!"

Ham took a deep breath. "Okay, no need to panic," he said to himself. "You're just hurtling out of a wormhole on the other side of the universe at nine-thousand miles per hour with no brakes."

"Aaaah!" Ham yelled. "Pull up! Pull up!" Frantically, he hit all the buttons on the ship.

"Oh, no," Ham mumbled to himself. Why hadn't he paid more attention during training?! "What was that landing sequence? Start the engines, true and fast, red one first, green one last. In between, press three, six, seven, or your next gig will be in heaven."

Poof! The landing bags deployed.

Ham looked out the window. "I did it! I did it!" he shouted. "I'm the smartest chimp in the universe."

But his joy was short-lived. *Boom!* The ship crash-landed on the planet.

And all Ham could do was scream.

CHAPTER SIX

Ham spun around inside the spaceship. He crashed into the control panel. He knocked his head on the floor. His butt smashed into the ceiling.

Finally, the ship stopped moving.

"Ship stabilized," a computerized voice said.

"That wasn't as bad as I thought," Ham said, breathing a sigh of relief.

Suddenly, the air bags deflated.

"Whoa!" Ham cried out as the ship started moving again.

Ham looked out the windshield. The ship was teetering on the edge of a cliff. Ham knew he needed to stay very still to keep the ship from going over the edge. But as soon as the ship had stopped rocking, Ham's nose began to itch. He held his breath, but it was too much. He sneezed so hard that it knocked him backward, and the ship fell over the edge. Ham screamed, but it was no use—the ship was falling and there was no one to help him.

Finally, the ship crashed at the bottom of the cliff. Everything was still for a moment. Then, suddenly, a roll of toilet paper fell out of the sky and landed squarely on top of the ship.

Back at mission control, the scientists hunched over their computers. They were trying to figure out where the ship was. They had lost communication when the ship went through the wormhole, and they hadn't been able to reestablish contact. The chimps' spaceship was nowhere in sight.

"You've lost the ship!" the senator yelled, banging his fist on a table.

Dr. Jagu tapped his screen. "It must be some sort of technical malfunction," he said.

The senator was irate. "Burning microwave popcorn is a technical malfunction. This is a billion-dollar disaster!" He couldn't believe how much money they had lost. How was he going to explain this to his voters? They were expecting the chimps' ship to blast into space and discover something fantastic—a new planet, aliens, anything! That would have made him a hero. But now the ship was gone, and his political career was doomed.

"We can always count on the twenty-four-hour fail-safe restart system," Dr. Poole spoke up.

The senator turned to face the doctor. "You have twenty-four hours to bring back those chimps, or I'll cut your funding and make this space program history. And I mean every cent. You won't even be able to afford pocket protectors." And with that, the senator stormed out of the room.

In the Simian Center, Houston and Comet were keeping a close eye out for the ship, too.

"They lost contact," Comet said worriedly.

Houston paced up and down, his eyes on the computer monitor.

Comet picked up his banana phone. "Comet to Luna," he said. "Come in, Luna."

There was no response.

"There must be some solar-flare interference," Comet reasoned. "I'll hack into the mainframe to filter the signal." And with that, he slipped into a vent and scurried off in search of the mainframe computer.

Ham peered through the porthole. "Great, we landed in Barstow. That settles it—we're firing our travel agent," he joked to himself.

He tried to open the hatch, but it was locked. What could he use to pick the lock? Suddenly, he had an idea—he could use his fingernails. Sure, they were dirty, but they were sharp. He slid a fingernail into the lock and voilà—the hatch opened!

Ham pulled himself out of the hatch and stepped onto the top rung of a ladder. "One small step for Ham!" he said as he carefully climbed down the ladder.

"And another small step, and another even smaller step, and . . ."

"What are you doing out there?" Luna cried from the hatch doorway.

Startled, Ham fell down the rest of the ladder.

When he hit the ground he looked up at Luna, who was standing at the top of the ship. "Testing for gravity," he joked. "Yup, it works! Nice to see that you finally woke up from your nap."

Luna was angry. "Who authorized you to open the hatch? It was specifically sealed before takeoff to prevent contamination. Commander!

Commander!" she called for Titan and then turned back to Ham with a scowl. "You're a liability to the mission," Luna continued.

"A liability?" Ham couldn't believe his ears. "*I* was steering this crate while you and Commander Coma were sawing logs!"

"You stayed awake, and you didn't activate the landing sequence?" Luna asked Ham. "That's all you had to do and you couldn't even do that right!"

"Not true," Ham countered. "I was catching up on my panicking."

Luna looked at the ship. The side of it was all scratched up. "I can't believe you crashed the ship," she said. "If you'd paid attention in training, this wouldn't have happened."

Ham rolled his eyes. He was hot and tired from the crash-landing and sick of Luna yelling at him. He pulled off his helmet and turned to go explore the planet, whether Luna liked it or not.

"No! Don't! Put your helmet back on," Luna cried. "The air could be poisonous. You need your helmet on for protection."

Ham's eyes got wide and he grabbed his throat with his hands, coughing and choking. "Oh, no. Poisonous air—choking," he gasped. Then he sank to the ground, still choking.

Luna rolled her eyes and took off her helmet, too. She hit a button on her watch and spoke into it: "Lieutenant's log—air is breathable. Temperature is normal."

But Ham was too busy acting to hear Luna's report. "Gasping, dying, winning Daytime Emmy," he said, crumpling to the ground.

Luna shook her head at Ham's performance. "And there's no sign of intelligent life," she said into her watch.

Pulling her eyes away from Ham, Luna looked up at the sky. The planet had three suns, and she thought she saw a flying creature swoop behind some clouds. A chill ran down her spine—whatever that thing was, it definitely was not your average bird!

Zartog's palace was complete, and he was pleased.

A sweet alien walked up to the evil ruler and handed him a bouquet of brightly colored flowers. "Your most omnipotent oppressor, please accept this bouquet from our village garden as a symbol of our unending servitude."

Zartog smiled. "For me? Oh, they're beautiful. Now all I need is a vase," he told the alien. Then with an evil glint in his eye, he said, "Say *ah*!"

The alien opened his mouth, and Zartog dipped him into the pool of freznar. When he pulled him out, Zartog put the flowers in the frozen alien's mouth. "You are a solid friend," Zartog said, patting the alien statue on the back with a smile.

Then Zartog turned to address the crowd. "As you all know, tomorrow is Triple Sunday. Our three suns will come together as one, and the volcano will explode. And in honor of this special day, and more importantly *me*, I'm throwing a celebration—a sort of palace-warming party. It'll be a great time for the newly enslaved to get to know one another."

The aliens didn't know what to say. They had no choice but to attend Zartog's party. Weakly, they all nodded their heads.

"Your prover, Lord!" someone shouted out.

Zartog turned his attention from the alien slaves. Who could be shouting at him? He looked up in the sky and saw an alien flying in on a fluvian. Fluvians were giant flying aliens that could be ridden through the sky. They were dangerous to ride, though, because if you pressed them in a certain spot poisonous darts would shoot out of their rumps, so only the bravest Malgorians attempted it.

"What?" Zartog asked impatiently.

"Another metal beast fell from the sky," the alien reported.

Zartog was shocked. "A metal beast? Like this one?" he asked, pointing to the prover.

The alien nodded. "Only bigger."

Zartog was furious. Anything bigger was probably better and more powerful than his prover. He had to get ahold of this new sky beast before someone else found it. Zartog pressed a button on the prover. The robotic arm shot out and lifted the alien into the air.

"Traitor!" Zartog shouted.

Zartog pressed another button on the prover, and the shocked alien was lowered into the freznar pool. Zartog smiled.

Then the smile faded from Zartog's face. What

if someone else found this new sky beast and tried to challenge his rule? They could start a rebellion. He could be defeated. Something had to be done—and fast.

Zartog turned to Splork and said, "Splork, congratulations, I am promoting you to general of my army. What's your strategy to capture the beast?"

Splork looked confused. Strategy? He didn't have a strategy. But he knew he had to say something fast. "Uh, say mean things to it. Call it stupid and ugly and kick it until it cries!"

"Bad answer," Zartog said, activating the prover's robotic arm.

"Stand at a safe distance while sending wave after wave of my men to subdue it," Splork said, thinking even faster. "Then bring it here and give you all of the credit, sir!"

Zartog nodded. "Yes, yes, that is good. Take

a party of warriors, and bring me back the sky beast!"

Splork chose a tall alien, an alien with a red belly, an alien wearing a pointy hat, and an alien with big splotches all over his body to join the team.

"Mount up," Splork commanded the warriors.

The aliens climbed on huge snail horses. They were ready to go.

"Take the fluvians!" Zartog shouted. He shook his head at their incompetence. How could they possibly expect to mount an attack against a sky beast riding snails?

Splork and his men climbed off the snails and mounted the fluvians. In seconds they were in the sky, off to capture the new sky beast!

CHAPTER SEVEN

"We're the first astronauts to ever set foot on this planet," Luna said, snapping a photo. "These photos will be front-page news—the most important news of the century!"

Just then, Ham popped up in front of the camera. "Can you get one of my good side?" he asked, posing like a supermodel. "Maybe take one of me looking heroic with my chin like this." Ham jutted his chin out and gave the camera a cheesy superhero grin.

Luna ignored him and turned the camera lens toward some flowers. She thought the beautiful pink and white flowers would make a lovely shot.

After taking the picture, she bent down to pick one of the flowers.

"I wouldn't do that if I were you," Ham cautioned her.

"This is the first sign of complex life on an alien planet," Luna said. "Astronauts gather knowledge. It's part of the mission. Scientists back on Earth will need to study samples of Malgorian flora and fauna."

Ham shrugged. "I'd just be a little careful," he said.

Luna laughed. "*You* careful? That's rich!"

"I'm just saying that looks like a flower used by Piddles the Clown," Ham responded.

Luna stood up and put her hands on her hips. "I've got to hear this. What exactly does space exploration have to do with a clown named Piddles?"

Ham explained that Piddles was a very cute

clown who had a cute little box that was covered with cute little flowers. Kids always thought that the box was the cutest thing they'd ever seen. But when they'd bend over to look at the box, a giant snake would pop out and scare them half to death!

Luna waved her hand in Ham's face. "Please, I'm a trained astronaut. I know what I'm doing."

Ham rolled his eyes. "Trained astronaut? We're nothing but Spam in a can. And we weren't even supposed to open the can. Space Chimps are a joke."

"Is that what you think of your grandfather?" Luna asked through gritted teeth.

Ham shot her an annoyed look. "Just pick your flowers and let's get back to Earth. If there's no traffic in the wormhole, I can still make the eight o'clock show at the circus."

Ham stormed back to the ship. "Uptight scientific bookworm lady," he muttered.

Luna watched him go. Then she bent down toward the flower.

Suddenly, a dozen thirty-foot-long snakes with shiny fangs popped up out of the ground and loomed over a terrified Luna.

"Ha-Ha-Ham, what does Piddles do next?" she stuttered.

Annoyed, Ham turned around. "Well, he usually throws a bucket of confetti on the snakes and then runs around in a circle really fast, smashing pies in his face. But I-I don't think this is going to help you here," he stammered as the snakes started to surround him as well. "Besides, I left the confetti and the pies on the ship. Yes, I brought pies. We'll just have to improvise."

Luna pulled her *Simian Space Manual* out from her pocket. "There must be something in here about what to do," she said, frantically flipping through the pages. "Alien captures, alien uprisings, how to say no to an alien probe . . . there's nothing about thirty-foot alien snakes!"

Ham had heard enough. He ran over to Luna and snatched the manual from her hands. Quickly, he tore up the book and threw it into the air like confetti.

And just like that, the snakes slithered away.

Ham smiled. "Confetti. I can't explain it. It just scares things."

But surprisingly, Luna still looked frightened. "Are you sure they're not scared of *them*?" she asked, pointing behind Ham.

Ham whirled around to see a giant alien army standing between him and Luna and the ship.

"Death to strangers!" Splork shouted.

"Great name for a band," Ham joked.

Wham! Spears flew through the air.

"Guess we aren't going to be best friends," Ham sighed.

Luna took off in the direction of the ship, shouting for Titan. "Commander! Wake up!"

But Ham grabbed her and pulled her away from the ship as spears rained down all around them. "Are you bananas?" he asked. "If we go back for Titan, we'll all be killed."

"But we can't just leave him or the ship," Luna said as Ham pushed her toward the edge of the nearby jungle.

Ham glanced behind him as he dodged another spear. The aliens were pulling the spaceship away. "It looks like they're leaving us," he replied.

Luna shook her head. "You should have never left the ship. This is all your fault," she told Ham. "Come on, we have to find out where they're taking Titan."

"*Me?* I didn't sign up for this! I should be in the makeup trailer right now, not stuck on an alien planet saving *you*!"

"*You* saving *me*?" Luna said incredulously. "That's a laugh."

Ham just rolled his eyes and kept running through the jungle. Suddenly, both chimps felt themselves slowing down. *Squish!* The ground underfoot was turning to mush.

"Wow, you are sinking really low," Ham joked.

"Yeah, well, you deserve it," Luna said, not realizing that they were actually sinking into the ground.

Just then they heard a noise overhead. "Look, the flying creatures are still after us. We have to get out of here!" Ham said, glancing up through the trees.

"I can't get out!" Luna said, struggling to free herself. She pulled one leg out, then the other. But there was nowhere to go. There was no solid ground in sight. "It's no use."

"Come on, like we say in the circus, 'The show

isn't over until the bearded lady shaves her back,'"
Ham said, trying to encourage her.

Luna sighed. "This isn't a circus."

"Life's a circus, Luna. Only the tents get bigger,"
Ham said.

Just then, darts rained down around them. Ham
knew he had to find a way out of there—and fast.
"Quick, climb on my shoulders and grab onto that
vine," he told Luna.

Luna climbed on Ham's shoulders and stood up.
Carefully, she grabbed the vine that was hanging
above her and pulled herself out of the muck. Then
Ham jumped up and onto her.

"Excuse me!" Luna exclaimed.

"Take it easy," Ham replied. "I'm staying alive
here, not monkeying around." Ham pulled himself
out of the muck and grabbed a nearby vine.

"Now what?" Luna asked.

"Swing," Ham told her. "Swing like the wind."

Ham easily swung over to the next vine and grabbed hold of it, pulling himself forward through the jungle. But when he looked back, Luna was still hanging on the first vine.

"Come on, Luna. Just pretend you're on a trapeze," Ham coached.

"I'm not from the circus!" Luna cried.

"You can do it. Release your inner chimp," Ham replied encouragingly.

Luna tried to swing her legs, but it was no use. She just couldn't reach the next vine.

Ham looked up to see the alien army closing in. In another minute, Ham and Luna would be captured! Quickly, Ham swung over to Luna and grabbed her hand. In one swift move, he pulled her back and threw her to the next vine.

"Taaaarrrzaaannn!" Ham yelled as they swung together on the vines. Luna quickly got the hang of swinging once Ham got her started. She was actually having fun! Soon, they were so deep in the jungle that the alien army could no longer see them from the sky.

"See," Ham said, as he swung from vine to vine. "Just a couple of chimps swinging through the jungle of vines with eyes and mouths."

Eyes and mouths?!

Ham screamed. "Vines don't have eyes and mouths!"

The vines opened their mouths and snapped their sharp teeth. They were trying to eat Ham and Luna!

Luckily, Ham had an idea. He pushed the head of the vine he was holding at the next vine. Ham's vine chomped the next vine right up, and Ham and Luna were able to keep swinging forward. Instead of trying to eat the chimps, the vines were eating each other!

Suddenly, Ham and Luna heard shouting

behind them. "There they are!" someone yelled.

Quickly, Ham turned around and saw the soldiers and their fluvians close behind. Ham kicked a vine into one of the alien's faces. *Snap!* The vine ate the alien in a flash.

Using the vines to fend off the army, Ham and Luna kept swinging through the forest. "Some first date?" Ham asked Luna jokingly.

"This is not a date," Luna said as she grabbed another vine.

"Oh, yes it is, and I really hope to see you again," Ham insisted.

"Will you stop?" Luna demanded, annoyed. Just a few more swings and they'd be out of the jungle. Luna counted the vines that were left: one, two, three . . .

Bright sunlight flooded their eyes. They had made it out of the jungle . . . only to find themselves hanging over a very deep canyon!

"Aaah!" Ham and Luna yelled as they fell.

Gum, cash, a cell phone, and a huge bunch of bananas flew out of Ham's pockets as he fell. As he tried to gather his stuff, he saw that Luna was spinning out of control. Ham went into a nosedive position and zoomed down next to Luna.

"I don't want to jinx it, but I think I'm falling for you," Ham said, swooping Luna into his arms.

"How can you make jokes at a time like this?" Luna asked frantically.

"Are you kidding me?" Ham said. "I do this every day of the week, except for Monday. That's my 'me-day.'"

Luna knew she had to trust Ham. That was the only way she was going to make it to the bottom of the canyon alive.

"Chin down, thumbs in!" Ham instructed.

Luna did as she was told, and incredibly, she started to fly in control! When it was time to land,

Ham told her to spread her arms wide, put her chin down, and aim for a soft patch he could see in the canyon.

As they came in for a landing, Ham did a few flips to show off. But Luna was concentrating hard—she didn't want to miss her target.

Suddenly, Ham gave her a shove, and *poof*— she landed safely on a giant mushroom.

Then, *boom*—Ham missed the target and slammed into the ground.

"We made it!" Luna cheered from on top of the mushroom. "Ham? Ham?" she called, looking around. But Ham wasn't on the mushroom with her. She crawled over to the edge and peered down below. Ham was lying on the ground next to the mushroom, and he wasn't moving!

CHAPTER EIGHT

"Ham, Ham! Get up!" Luna cried as she climbed off the mushroom and ran to Ham's side. "You're okay, right? Come on, Ham." She leaned over Ham, but he didn't even stir.

"I'm so sorry I was rough on you," Luna said kindly, her eyes closed as she leaned over Ham's limp form. "Sure, you were irresponsible, dangerous, and undisciplined, but you saved my life. And you were kind of funny in an unbelievably annoying way. And you were even . . ."

"Cute?" Ham cut in.

"No," Luna said. She was so upset that she didn't even realize that Ham was okay.

"Handsome?" Ham continued, with his eyes still closed.

"No," Luna said, still not catching on.

"Like Brad Pitt, but way shorter and more hairy?" Ham joked.

Luna opened her eyes and looked down to see Ham grinning up at her. "Ugh!" she yelled. She was glad he was all right, but she was annoyed he had tricked her like that.

Back at the Space Center, Comet plugged the banana phone into the lab's super computer. Urgently, he typed some equations on the keyboard. Houston paced back and forth as Comet worked, hoping that the genius chimp could make contact with the others.

Finally, the banana phone crackled to life. "Luna, do you copy? Come in, Luna," Comet said.

"Let me just say one thing." Comet and Houston

heard Luna's voice come in over the phone.

"She's alive!" Comet shouted.

Luna continued talking. "You are the most annoying, obnoxious, self-centered creature I have ever met!"

"Ham's alive, too!" Houston shouted, realizing that Luna had to be talking about his little friend— no one else pushed her buttons like Ham!

"Luna, Ham, do you read me?" Comet said into the phone. "Come in."

But there was no response.

"We can hear them, but they can't hear us," Houston concluded.

Comet started typing again on the keyboard. "We'll need to calibrate the Gregorian array, replace the helix mirror, and cross-feed the surrounding shroud."

Houston shook his head. "The only word I understood was *feed*."

While Houston and Comet were working, Luna was storming through the canyon, ignoring Ham as best she could. "Mission log, we are stranded on a hostile alien planet," she spoke into her watch. "Commander Titan has been kidnapped and . . ."

"We're falling in love," Ham leaned in to speak into the watch.

"No, we're not," Luna quickly countered. "Ignore that last part. Delete! Delete!"

Luna continued. "We have lost our ship and have only seventeen hours before the automatic pilot engages and we're stuck here forever."

"What do you mean stuck?" Ham asked.

"The ship has a built-in safety program to automatically fly back to Earth twenty-four hours after we land, in the event something happened to us. It was in your manual," Luna explained.

"Was that before or after the chapter on the

fleet of rescue ships they'll send to save us?" Ham asked.

Luna shook her head. "We've got one chance of getting home."

"I've had worse odds that that," Ham said. "Let's get moving."

The chimps' spaceship was causing quite the scene back at Zartog's palace. Zartog stood at the top of its ladder as he addressed the crowd of alien slaves below. "Behold Sky Beast Two, the sequel!"

The aliens stared at the ship. It was larger than the prover, which meant that Zartog was even more powerful than before. The aliens shook with fear.

"Yes, let the fear course through your yellow blood!" Zartog said with a snicker.

"Greetings, aliens!" a voice called out from behind Zartog.

Zartog turned around to see a huge chimp

standing in the doorway of the spaceship, his mouth opened wide in a huge yawn.

"Aaah!" Zartog screamed as he tumbled down the ladder to the ground.

"Don't worry," Titan said cheerfully. "You didn't wake me. I needed to get up."

Zartog's eyes grew wide with fear. Who was this strange creature, and what did he want? Would he threaten Zartog's rule?

Titan cleared his throat. "I am Commander Titan."

A hush fell over the crowd as Titan spoke.

"I have traveled through space in search of knowledge and to explore the outer reaches of the universe. I am pleased to make first contact with aliens like yourselves, seal you in Mylar wrap, and take you to my home planet to be dissected."

"Dissected?" Zartog asked. What was this creature talking about?

"Oh, you know," Titan said with a knowing smile. "It's where we lay you down on some nice wax paper, slice you open, and poke around in your insides. But first you'll need to form a line so I can label and catalog you."

Titan pulled out a sheet of labels from his pocket. He walked down the ladder and moved through the crowd, placing a label on each alien he passed.

"Organism number one," he said as he stuck a label on a tall purple alien. Then he turned to a short blue alien and stuck another label on him. "Organism number two."

Then Zartog stepped in Titan's way.

"Ah! Organism number three," Titan said, filling out a new label.

"I am Lord Zartog," Zartog growled as Titan slapped a label on him. "I am the ruler of Planet Malgor."

Titan stopped to consider Zartog. He looked

into his beady red eyes and said, "Zartog, eh? Your parents named you that? Is that with one *g* or two?"

Zartog growled.

"I'll take that as a one," Titan said. He wrote a new label and stuck it over the old one on Zartog's chest. Then, Titan turned to another alien. "Organism number four, organism number five, organ—"

Suddenly, Titan felt something grab him around the waist. He looked down and saw that he was being held by the prover's robotic arm. It lifted him up off the ground.

"Whoa there, mister!" Titan shouted. "That's Space Agency property. You're in direct violation of interstellar protocol. But if you cooperate with me, I will ask the tribunal to go easy on you."

"Cooperate with *you*?" Zartog snorted. "I'm going to destroy you."

"I appreciate your honesty. You're a good man,

Zartog, and a worthy adversary. Be proud," Titan said.

Zartog moved Titan toward the dunking pool. Suddenly, the robotic arm jerked back and forth.

"Ha!" Titan shouted triumphantly. "You don't even know how to use the reticulating micro movement device. Even a first-year cadet knows that."

Zartog pressed several buttons and managed to get the arm under control. "Will you show me the secrets of the beast?" he asked Titan.

"Negative!" Titan shouted. There was no way he would teach a non-Space Agency-certified creature how to operate the spaceship.

Zartog's face fell. He had to learn how to work the beast. It would give him what he needed— ultimate power. "I'll do anything," he pleaded.

Titan thought for a moment. "You could help me find my crew," he said slowly.

"There are more of you?" Zartog asked with panic in his voice.

Just then, Splork walked over. "Two others," he announced. "We lost them in Gunglevik Jungle."

Zartog laughed. "What kind of idiot would go in there?"

Titan knew exactly what kind of an idiot—Ham!

CHAPTER NINE

Malgor's second sun was setting, and the hills were awash in a beautiful blue glow. Ham looked out at the alien skyline and felt a sense of calm.

"I have to admit that being on a weird alien planet is kind of nice," he said.

"Kind of?" Luna asked.

"Well, the fact that we were nearly killed by vicious aliens did put a damper on things. But then again, I'm a pessimist," Ham said.

Luna watched the red and gold light reflect off the canyon walls. She was so proud of herself. "All my life I looked up at the picture of your grandfather and dreamed of being a real astronaut just like him, and here I am," she told Ham.

"Real astronauts?" Ham said, laughing. "Wake up, Luna. The only reason we're here is to see if we explode in space."

"You're wrong. We're real astronauts," Luna replied, walking away.

Ham ran to catch up with her. "This mission was a one-way ticket from the start. That's why they sent us."

Luna shook her head. "They sent us because chimps go first."

They walked in silence for a few minutes. As the darkness settled around them, Ham felt it was time to tell Luna the truth. He told her that they were being used as an experiment. The humans didn't care if they lived.

Just then, Ham thought he saw a flicker of light out of the corner of his eye. When Ham turned to investigate, the light moved!

Ham soars over the circus.

Ham I—the first chimp in space.

Ham III—stunt chimp extraordinaire.

Ham and Houston

Ham sends Titan flying during training.

The Space Agency scientists study the Space Chimps.

Malgor

One small step for Chimp-kind.

Fluvian attack

Kilowatt

Ham groovin' with the globhoppers and Kilowatt.

Zartog loses control of the prover.

Ham and Luna to the rescue.

Building the *Chimpfinity*

Ham crash-lands the *Chimpfinity* right on target.

The aliens of Malgor say good-bye to the Space Chimps.

The Space Agency scientists are shocked by the chimps' return.

"Okay, which one of us lost our flashlights?" Ham asked. Then the light moved again. Ham and Luna followed the flickering light until it disappeared behind some rocks. When they turned the corner they saw a small creature with a glowing head.

"Please, I-I mean you no harm," the creature said, shaking.

"Ditto. I am Lieutenant Luna. We are your friends," Luna said encouragingly.

The creature still seemed afraid. "M-my name is Killawallaaizzaseywhoha," she said. "I'm the last free Luzian from the village of Killawallawazoowahooweeeee."

"We'll call you Kilowatt," Luna said, trying to make the creature feel comfortable. "We come from Earth."

The creature did not understand what Luna had said. She just shook her head, causing light to bounce off the canyon walls.

"You know, Earth?" Ham said. "Big Macs, iTunes, David Beckham, Dave Matthews Band. Any of these ringing a bell?"

Kilowatt glowed brightly.

"Whoa!" Ham said, shielding his eyes. "What's with the glow-in-the-dark brain case?"

"My head lights up when I am scared," Kilowatt explained.

"You don't need to be scared of us," Luna said kindly. "We're your friends."

Kilowatt smiled, and her head glowed warmly.

"Are you alone?" Luna asked.

Kilowatt nodded and told them that everyone from her village had been captured by Zartog and his sky beast. She went on to explain that the sky beast's metal claws gave Zartog the power to enslave the entire planet.

As Kilowatt described the sky beast's shiny hide and long metal arms and claws, Luna realized that the sky beast Kilowatt was talking about was the prover from the *Infinity* probe.

"We, too, came from the stars," Luna told Kilowatt.

Kilowatt nodded. "Yes, I saw you crash."

"I did that!" Ham said proudly.

"Do you know where our ship is?" Luna wanted to know.

"It's at Zartog's palace," Kilowatt said.

Ham and Luna wanted Kilowatt to take them there, but Kilowatt was afraid. She was scared that Zartog would capture her, like he did the rest of the Luzians. But Luna promised that she and Ham would protect the little alien. So Kilowatt agreed to help.

"We will set off in the morning," Kilowatt said. "Now we should sleep. The journey to Zartog's palace is perilous. We must cross through the Valley of Very Bad Things."

"You should work harder on some of the names

around here," Ham said. "How about Sugar Land, or Cotton Candy Valley, or I Feel Good Mountains?"

"It's a land of untold danger, agony, and torture," Kilowatt continued. "Not to mention avian urk flu, death spouts, mad florg disease, and the Cave of the Flesh-Devouring Beast."

Luna was concerned. "Do we *have* to take the Valley of Very Bad Things?"

"Well, there is the Valley of Very, Very, Very, Very, Very Bad Things. It's a bit shorter, but, honestly, not worth the time we'd save," Kilowatt said with a smile.

Kilowatt looked up. The third sun had set, leaving the sky pitch black. The only light came from her head. "Sleep," she told Ham and Luna. "You will need your rest."

Ham and Luna lay down on the ground and shut their eyes. It felt nice to rest. Kilowatt was right—some sleep would do them good.

But, five seconds later, Kilowatt shouted, "Up! Wake!"

Ham and Luna opened their eyes. The three suns had risen. It was a bright, sunny day.

"Well, that was refreshing," Ham said sarcastically. "We were only asleep for like . . ."

"Five seconds," Luna continued, looking at her watch.

Kilowatt smiled. "That's just one of the benefits of living on a planet with three suns."

"And my solar-powered calculator still doesn't work," Ham said with a sigh.

"Follow me," Kilowatt said, starting to walk.

Luna lifted her watch to her mouth. "Mission log—I have good news and bad news. We're being guided to our ship by a friendly alien who we have named Kilowatt, but Commander Titan's status is still unknown."

Kilowatt led Ham and Luna through a canyon.

Colorful fruit grew out of the cracks in the walls. As Ham walked, he picked the fruit and popped it into his mouth.

"Wow, these are even better than circus peanuts," he commented.

Luna shook her head. "I still can't believe the grandson of the great Ham works at a circus."

"Hey, I like what I do," Ham said defensively. "And just because my grandfather was who he was, why does everyone expect me to follow in his footsteps?" He put another piece of fruit in his mouth.

"Don't you want to be a hero?" Luna asked.

Ham shook his head. "I just want to be me. For the longest time I wished my parents hadn't even named me Ham. I mean, why couldn't they have picked some other regular old chimp name, like Coco, or Bongo, or Derek?"

Kilowatt plucked two unusual-looking pieces

of fruit from the wall and handed them to Ham. "Here, try this snizzlefruit."

"Mmmm," Ham said, stuffing the fruit in his mouth. "Tastes like caramel apple with a subtle hint of pizza bagel. You wouldn't think it, but they go."

"I wish I could have welcomed you with fruit from our village, but sadly, Zartog destroyed everything," Kilowatt said.

Then Kilowatt asked Ham and Luna why they made the prover. It was such a beast—so destructive.

Luna explained that they didn't make the prover; humans did.

"What are humans?" Kilowatt asked.

"They're like us," Luna explained. "Well, ninety-nine-point-nine percent like us."

Ham picked up a piece of fruit with his feet and ate it. "That point-one percent makes all the difference. After all, have you seen a human who can eat with his feet? Didn't think so!"

Ham picked up another piece of fruit and started to take a bite.

"Stop, don't!" Kilowatt shouted.

Ham took the fruit away from his mouth and looked at it. "But I love gumdrops," he said disappointedly.

"That's not food," Kilowatt explained. "That's a globhopper." She told Ham that globhoppers were little aliens that copied your every move.

Ham put the globhopper down on the ground and started to dance. Sure enough, the globhopper started to dance, too! Then more globhoppers came along to join in the fun.

Luna couldn't believe her eyes. "Why any life-form would want to mimic you is one of the unsolved mysteries of the universe," she said.

Ham ignored Luna's remark and tried to get

her to dance, too. At first she refused, saying that chimps don't dance. But soon she admitted that she'd never danced before—she didn't even know how!

Ham grabbed Luna's arm and twirled her around. In no time at all, Luna was dancing—and she was having fun.

Suddenly, Ham grabbed his butt and cried out in pain. All the globhoppers grabbed their butts, too! A dart had hit him right in the rear.

Wham! Wham! Wham! More fluvian darts rained down from the sky. They were under attack!

CHAPTER TEN

"Fluvian fighters!" Kilowatt shouted as she and Ham and Luna started to run.

But they couldn't run fast enough to get away from the fluvians, who were quickly gaining on them, and there was nowhere to hide in the canyon. Suddenly, Ham had an idea. As the darts fell from the sky, he did a cartwheel. At first, Luna thought he was just fooling around, as usual, but then the globhoppers started to mimic him. The mimicking globhoppers formed a wheel. Ham jumped inside the wheel and started running.

"Man, I love these dudes. Jump in!" he called to Luna and Kilowatt.

Ham reached out and grabbed his friends. With a loud screech, the wheel took off, with Ham, Luna, and Kilowatt running inside. They looked as if they were running on a treadmill!

"They don't call me the Hamster for nothing," Ham joked.

The wheel sped across the ground, leaving the fluvians in its dust.

Ham turned to Luna and said, "Well, I have to say that no one is ever going to take you on a better first date than this."

"Stop calling it a date," Luna said, annoyed. "This is a mission." Luna looked down. She was holding Ham's hand! Horrified, she quickly pulled her hand away. Then she took his hand back.

"I-I was monitoring your pulse," Luna weakly tried to explain.

Ham smiled. "Oh, good idea—I need constant medical attention."

"Your heart is beating a little fast," Luna said.

"That's because you're holding my hand," Ham replied.

Quickly, Luna dropped his hand again and concentrated on outrunning the fluvians. After a while, she looked up at the empty sky. "I think we lost them," she said.

"Man, am I glad we didn't eat these guys," Ham said gratefully, looking at the globhoppers.

Suddenly, the wheel broke apart, sending Ham, Luna, and Kilowatt flying into the air.

"We really have to work on stopping, though," Ham said after he crash-landed. He looked around for the globhoppers and saw them racing away. "No, wait—don't leave, gumdrop people! Your stopping skills are great! You're the best gumdrop-wheel-stoppers I've ever seen!" Ham shook his head. "Man, they're sensitive."

"They are afraid," Kilowatt explained. "It's

the Cave of the Flesh-Devouring Beast."

Luna and Ham looked at the dark cave that loomed in front of them.

"What's with this planet? Would it kill you to have a Cave of Sweet Little Kittens?" Ham asked.

Suddenly, the fluvians appeared overhead again. They had caught up!

"Looks like we have no choice but to go into that cave," Luna said as the darts fell around them.

"You're right," Ham agreed. "I'm so scared that we should probably hold hands again." He took hold of Luna's hand.

"Please," Luna said, pushing Ham away. "I'm not holding hands."

Just then, darts whizzed past her head. She grabbed onto Ham's hand, and they dashed into the cave behind Kilowatt.

The inside of the cave was dark and creepy-looking. A wet chill hung in the air.

"Maybe we'll get lucky and this beast will only devour our flesh with his eyes," Ham said as they walked.

Just then, Kilowatt's head lit up, illuminating their surroundings. Standing right in front of them was the Flesh-Devouring Beast! The creature had brown slimy skin and rows and rows of razor-sharp teeth. The beast let out a terrifying roar, sending Ham, Luna, and Kilowatt literally running for their lives.

The beast chased them through the cave, snapping and snarling. As they ran, Kilowatt's head glowed brighter and brighter, until Ham and Luna were blinded by the light. They couldn't see the way out!

"Kilowatt, turn yourself off!" Ham shouted.

"I can't," Kilowatt replied. "I'm too scared!"

"But if we can't get out of here, we're dead!" Luna reasoned.

"That is not helping!" Kilowatt said, glowing even brighter.

Up ahead, Ham saw some rocks. He led the group there, and they tried to hide. "Here's a trick to control your fear," Ham whispered to Kilowatt. "Imagine what you're most afraid of in the world, and then imagine overcoming it."

"What would *you* know about control?" Luna asked.

But as soon as she asked the question, Kilowatt's light started to go out.

"Wow, it works! Thank you, Ham. I've been scared my entire life, and I never knew how to control it."

Luna was impressed. "Where did you learn that?" she asked.

"Houston. He taught me everything I know," Ham answered proudly.

Now that Kilowatt's light was off, the group

was safe behind the rocks. But, they were also trapped—the Flesh-Devouring Beast was still waiting for them. They heard the monster sniffing around. It was trying to pick up their scent. Ham imagined the beast licking its teeth, waiting for its next meal. How could they escape?

"Please free my planet from the evil Zartog," Kilowatt whispered sincerely.

Ham was nervous. What was Kilowatt doing?

Slowly, Kilowatt's light turned back on. In horror, Ham and Luna watched their little friend run through the beast's legs. As the beast gave chase, Kilowatt said, "If you strike me down, I will only grow stronger."

The beast opened his mouth, and the cave was plunged into darkness once more. Kilowatt was gone.

CHAPTER ELEVEN

Ham and Luna ran out of the cave.

"Kilowatt, why?" Ham said with tears in his eyes. "She was so brave. Now I see what it means to be a hero."

Luna sat down on the ground and placed her head in her hands. "Bravery like that isn't covered in a manual." She sighed and then continued. "I've spent my whole life training to be an astronaut, and for what? Hours on that treadmill—what were we supposed to do, jog in space? I'm sick of living by the book. What's it ever gotten me?"

"At least you didn't have to grow up in your famous grandpa's shadow."

Luna looked at Ham. "How does that make you feel?"

Ham thought for a moment before responding. "Cold. Do you know what it's like to live in a shadow? It's cold in that shadow. I knew I could never become a hero, so I became a clown."

Luna didn't speak. Now she understood Ham. He wasn't just a goofy chimp. There was more to him. All his life he was compared to his grandfather. That had to have been difficult. She smiled and stood up. It was time to get on with the mission. They had to find Titan and their spaceship before the fail-safe restart system was activated.

The three suns were starting to come together over the volcano, and they cast a spooky glow on Zartog's palace, where all of his alien slaves were gathered. Zartog sat on the prover overlooking the crowd.

"Pathetic groveling slaves of Malgor, welcome to Triple Sunday," Zartog said.

"Soon the suns will align, and the volcano will explode. A lot of you are not going to live. Others will be dunked. But, on the plus side, there will be free pudding and balloons for the kids."

Splork walked through the crowd whispering, "Smile or dunk. Smile or dunk." Obediently the aliens smiled, making Zartog think they were genuinely happy.

"Now it is my thrill to present the main attraction—the chimp who showed me the way to make your lives even more miserable. Here's Titan!"

Zartog pressed a button on the prover, and the robotic arm rose. Hanging from its metal claws was Titan! Zartog pressed another button, and Titan was lowered toward the dunking pool.

"Now that I've gotten to know you, you seem

like a reasonable alien," Titan said. "Which is why I'm willing to offer you a plea bargain."

Zartog shook his head.

"How about a written warning and a small fine?" Titan continued.

While Titan was trying to figure out a way to save himself, Ham and Luna had reached the palace.

"Whoa—this place is huge!" Ham said, marveling at the gaudy palace.

"It must cost a fortune to air-condition in the summer," Luna said with a smile.

Ham turned to her with a surprised look. "I thought a sense of humor was against regulations."

"What are you going to do? Chimp-martial me?" Luna asked teasingly.

Ham laughed and turned his gaze back to the crowd of aliens. It was creepy how they were all smiling. What was going on down there?

"Oh, my gosh—Titan!" Luna suddenly shouted when she spotted him dangling over the dunking pool.

Luna and Ham knew they had to save their commander, but how? If they had their rocket packs, they'd be able to swoop in and rescue him. Sadly, their packs were in the ship.

Thinking hard and fast, Luna spotted the fluvians tied up in a corral. Recognizing them as the flying creatures the aliens had chased them on, Luna had an idea. Quickly, she led Ham down the hill toward the corral.

Ham and Luna each untied a fluvian, jumped on, and held them by their long, handlebar-like ears.

"Right ear, stop, left ear go!" Ham shouted, figuring out how to fly the creatures. "Follow me, Luna!"

Down at the freznar pool, Titan was still trying to talk his way out of getting dunked. "Go ahead," he told Zartog. "Dunk me. Now you'll never learn how to use the 3-D radar."

"3-D radar?" Zartog asked.

"That's right. Flip the bar with the star, not too far, to start the radar," Titan explained.

Zartog followed the instructions. Suddenly, laser beams spread out around the prover, and an alarm sounded.

"Alert! Chimpanzees are incoming!" A computerized voice shrilled.

Zartog looked up and saw the fluvians swooping in toward Titan. "Traitors!" he shouted. In one swift move, Zartog grabbed Ham off the fluvian.

"Aha! I've captured another one!" Zartog shouted triumphantly.

"You hardly captured me," Ham said. "I mean, I just showed up here on my own."

Zartog shook his head. "What's with your species? Give credit where credit is due! To the dunk!"

"Yes, to the dunk!" Ham echoed. "What's the dunk?"

Seeing that Ham was captured, Luna kicked her fluvian. Darts shot out, one landing in Zartog's shoulder.

"Ouch!" Zartog cried, dropping Ham.

Ham fell toward the dunking pool. But in the last second, Luna swooped in and caught him.

"My hero!" Ham shouted.

Together, they flew to Titan, who had wriggled free of the prover's claws. Titan jumped on the fluvian, and the three chimps flew off. Luna kicked the fluvian again, and a hail of darts rained down on Splork and his men.

"Traitors! Traitors!" Zartog yelled as the aliens cheered.

Quickly, the chimps flew to their ship and ran inside.

"I can see the headlines now," Titan said as

Ham closed the hatch. "'Commander Titan returns to Earth.' What will I wear? I mean, what goes with ticker tape?"

"Sir, launch control is unresponsive!" Luna reported.

"Check diagnostics!" Titan commanded.

Luna opened the console. Her eyes widened—there was nothing inside! Why were they taught how to operate the ship if the controls were never hooked up? Ham had been right all along—the whole mission was a scam. The ship had been on autopilot the whole time. The chimps were never really flying it. They were never really astronauts. The scientists just wanted to see if their brains still worked after going through a wormhole. They were nothing more than guinea pigs.

"Three minutes to liftoff," the ship's voice announced. The twenty-four-hour time limit was up and the ship was about to return to Earth automatically. The chimps didn't have to do anything.

Ham looked out the window. Zartog was threatening the Luzians with the prover's arms. "I can't go," he said flatly.

"What?" Luna asked.

"I know we didn't build the *Infinity* probe, but it came from Earth. We did this to them. I can't run away. We owe it to Kilowatt, and to the planet."

Luna considered what Ham said. "Ham's right. I'd rather be a hero here on Malgor than a space chump back on Earth."

But Titan wasn't buying it. "I took an oath to return this ship to Earth, and that's what I'm going to do."

"Good luck, Commander," Luna said.

"Lieutenant, stay in the ship," Titan ordered.

"Sorry, but that's one order I can't obey," Luna answered.

"One minute to liftoff," the ship's voice said.

Hearing that, Luna and Ham jumped out of the ship.

The ship's engines rumbled to life. The sky filled with smoke. Ham and Luna watched as the rocket rose above the smoke and blasted into space.

"There goes our ride," Ham commented.

"And Titan," Luna added.

The chimps just stood there watching the ship disappear in the sky. Suddenly, they saw Titan walking through the smoke toward them!

Ham and Luna couldn't believe their eyes. What was he doing there? What happened to his oath?

"Chimps don't leave chimps behind," Titan explained.

Luna smiled. Then she turned to Ham. "We need a plan."

Ham looked at the prover. "We have to take that thing out!"

"Um, the commander of the mission comes up with the plan," Titan said.

"And your plan is?" Luna wanted to know.

But Titan did not know what to say. And as he stumbled for his words, Zartog sneaked up behind him and grabbed him with the prover's claws.

"It's party time!" Zartog shouted with an evil smile.

CHAPTER TWELVE

Back on Earth, the scientists were in the rocket garden, eagerly awaiting the return of the ship. They knew that the twenty-four-hour fail-safe start had activated, but were the chimps still alive inside?

"We have contact," Dr. Jagu reported. "The ship has exited the wormhole."

"Touchdown in fifteen seconds," Dr. Poole added.

The senator turned to the group of reporters gathered in the garden. "Roll the cameras," he said from the podium. As soon as the rocket landed, he was going to deliver his victory speech.

At last the ship landed. A cheer went up from

the crowd. Reporters snapped their cameras.

The scientists rushed up to the ship. But all they found inside was a fiery, smoky mess.

"I'm afraid the chimpanzees did not make it," Dr. Jagu said, hanging his head.

"You think?" Dr. Bob said sarcastically.

The senator banged his hands on the podium. "That's it! Mission canceled! The space program is done. As of tomorrow, this entire agency will be recommissioned into something useful, like one of those places where you design, paint, and bake your own plates."

"What about the two chimps still here?" Dr. Smothers asked.

"Two chimps, two words—animal testing," the senator said with a scowl.

Inside the Simian Center, Comet and Houston knew it was time to get to work. Thanks to Comet's banana phones, they knew that Luna, Ham, and Titan were still on Planet Malgor. Comet put his computer into his backpack and started to climb into the vent.

"Hold on!" Houston shouted, mischievously looking at the rocket packs. The one Ham had worn was dented and burned. But the other two were in perfect condition.

Just then, two guards kicked in the door of the Simian Center. Quickly, Houston and Comet slipped on the rocket packs. As the guards threw their nets, the chimps pressed the start buttons.

"Houston, for a twentieth-century chimp, you're moving pretty quickly into the twenty-first century," Comet said.

Houston and Comet lifted off, and the room filled with smoke. They shot right into the air ducts. As they passed the ceiling, the rockets set off the fire sprinklers, drenching the guards.

"I may be old," Houston said, "but I'm aerodynamic!"

Things weren't looking good on Malgor. Zartog had Titan, Luna, and Ham grasped in the prover's robotic arm over a pool of bubbling freznar.

"At last," Zartog said triumphantly. "Prepare to be dunked."

"As commander, the least I can do is make sure Zelbaum here doesn't dunk you guys," Titan said to Luna and Ham.

"Ha! And why would I do that?" Zartog asked.

Titan smiled. "Because I will teach you the prover's universal domination sequence."

That sounded interesting to Zartog. If he knew the sequence, then he could conquer the entire universe!

"Fine," Zartog said after a moment. "If you tell me the sequence I will let your friends go."

"All right. Let them go first, and then I'll tell you," Titan agreed.

"No, Titan, you can't!" Luna cried as Zartog released her and Ham.

"I'm sorry, Luna, but I have to save you and Ham. To dominate the universe," Titan began, turning to Zartog, "hit the yellow button first, turn the blue knob, then the green knob, and pull the lever in reverse."

Zartog hit the keys with a greedy smile on his face. As soon as he pulled the lever, Zartog was shot out of his seat. He flew through the air and landed right in the dunking pool!

Titan had told Zartog the eject sequence. A cheer went up from the aliens. They were free from the evil Zartog! As Ham scanned the crowd, his eyes fell upon a familiar face.

"Kilowatt?" Ham said. "You're alive!"

Kilowatt bobbed her head up and down.

"But how? We saw the Flesh-Devouring Beast swallow you," Luna said.

"Lucky for me, he didn't chew," Kilowatt answered with a shy smile.

"But how did you get out?" Ham wanted to know.

Kilowatt blushed. "I'd rather not talk about it," she said.

Ham and Luna helped Titan out of the prover's claw, and then they all turned to face the crowd of aliens.

"You have liberated us from the bonds of slavery!" Kilowatt said gratefully. "We are eternally grateful. We owe you our lives." Everyone cheered in agreement.

Titan jumped on the prover and fished Zartog out of the pool with the robotic arm. He was a statue, and he could never hurt anyone again! Splork put a party hat on him, and the crowd celebrated.

In the middle of the celebration, Ham heard a ringing sound. He looked over at Titan. "Uh, your banana is ringing."

Luna picked up the banana phone. Comet was on the other end.

"Guys, can you hear me?" Comet asked.

"You'll never believe what's been happening," Luna said excitedly.

But Comet told her that he and Houston were able to hear everything the whole time. He explained that they were lucky they weren't on the ship—they would have never made it through the wormhole alive. The humans had miscalculated the reentry angle.

Then Houston got on the phone with Ham and told him that the senator had shut down the entire space program.

"Then where are you?" Ham wanted to know.

"Mission control!" Houston replied. "And we're

ready to help guide you home."

"In what?" Ham asked. "Our ship's gone. There's nothing to guide."

"But you still have the probe," Houston said.

Titan, Luna, and Ham looked at the probe. What was Houston talking about? The probe was not designed to return to Earth.

Titan shrugged. "I guess we'll have to chimprovise!" he said.

"Titan's right," Houston said. "You'll need a complete redesign."

Comet took the phone from Houston and explained what to do. He told Luna they had to reengineer the aerodynamic skeletal structure. They also needed thrust—at least sixteen-million meganewtons.

"There's no way," Luna said, after listening to Comet's instructions. "We just can't create that kind of thrust. We don't have fuel."

But Ham had an idea. "If you can launch a chimp out of a cannon, we can fire a ship out of a volcano."

That was it! The suns were about to align. Once they did, the volcano would erupt. And when the volcano erupted, it would provide enough force to shoot them into space. But they had to complete the ship and get it into position before the volcano erupted.

"We don't have a lot of time," Luna said, looking up at the sky.

"Let's chimp this ride!" Titan said.

Luna turned to Kilowatt and said, "We're going to need some help if we're ever going to get home."

Kilowatt bowed. "Planet Malgor, at your service!"

CHAPTER THIRTEEN

With the help of the aliens, the chimps built a ship out of the probe. Fluvians lifted and carried metal tubes from the aqueduct. Kilowatt and the other Luzians provided work lights. And Titan lifted heavy metal panels onto the ship.

"Well, she won't win any beauty contests, but she'll fly," Ham said, looking at the ship.

"Okay, you just need one more piece," Comet instructed. "You need a nose cone to safely penetrate the Earth's atmosphere."

Splork and his soldiers had the perfect idea— Zartog! They lifted the Zartog statue and placed him on the front of the new ship.

The volcano rumbled. The planet shook. The suns aligned in the sky. It was time for liftoff!

Titan, Ham, and Luna said good-bye to Kilowatt, and thanked all the aliens for their help. The aliens were grateful, too. Now, when the volcano erupted, all the freznar would be used to launch the spaceship instead of freezing their village. And the spaceship wouldn't freeze, because the heat from the engines would deactivate the freznar. It was a perfect plan!

The aliens positioned the new ship in the mouth of the volcano.

"Let's light this candle!" Ham shouted from inside the ship.

Luna covered her eyes. "I can't bear to look!"

There was a loud rumbling sound. "It's louder than a cannon," Ham said, covering his ears.

"I think I'm going to be sick!" Titan said, covering his mouth.

Boom! The volcano erupted, and the chimps blasted off!

Luna and Titan worked the controls as the spaceship hurtled toward the wormhole. As they came closer, Titan passed the controls to Ham.

"I can't do this," Ham said, pushing the controls away.

"You have to," Titan pleaded. "When we pass out, you've got to pilot us home."

"I can't," Ham said, shaking his head. "I'm not an astronaut."

"Are you wearing aluminum clothes?" Titan asked.

"Yes," Ham said.

"Are you in a rocket?"

Ham nodded.

"In outer space?"

"Yeah," Ham said.

"Are you David Bowie?" Titan asked.

"No," Ham replied, puzzled.

"Then you must be an astronaut," Titan said, giving Ham a playful push. "Now bring this bird home, hotshot." And with that, Titan passed out.

Ham took the controls. But he was still worried. In the circus, he always missed the target. What would happen if he missed now? He shuddered thinking about the answer. Ham was afraid.

"Here's a trick," Luna said, trying to help. "To control your fear, imagine what you're most afraid of, and then imagine overcoming it."

"I appreciate the effort, I really do, but you're forgetting one thing—*I am an idiot!*" Ham said.

"Ham," Luna said as bursts of light penetrated the ship. "I believe in you," Luna said, closing her eyes.

"Wait, Luna—no!" Ham cried.

But it was too late, Luna passed out just as the ship was sucked into the wormhole.

And all Ham could do was scream.

CHAPTER
FOURTEEN

Ham fought to stay awake. He had to guide the ship safely through the wormhole. Colors and images danced in front of his eyes. Ham even thought he saw his grandfather, Ham I, looking down on him.

"Believe in yourself," Ham's grandfather said.

"I can't do this, I'm not you," Ham said.

"Well, of course you're not me, you're you. You can do things—just do them your way, " his grandfather answered and gave him a thumbs-up.

With renewed determination, Ham grabbed the controls and stabilized the ship as it exited the wormhole.

"Ham, you're coming in too hot," Comet said over the phone. "You've got to reduce your angle for reentry by exactly thirty-three degrees."

"Kind of exactly or exactly exactly?" Ham asked.

"Exactly exactly. If you don't nail that reentry window, you'll be space dust," Comet told him.

Ham used his hands and feet to adjust the buttons on the control panel. Then he engaged the ailerons, flicked the turbulence coolers on, adjusted the heat deflectors, and enabled the gyroscopic stabilizers.

As Ham struggled to operate all the buttons, he heard a voice: "Need a copilot?"

Ham breathed a sigh of relief—Luna was awake!

"Mission control, adjusting angle to thirty-three degrees," Ham reported.

"Entering Earth's atmosphere," Luna added. "Prepare for burn-in."

Ham worked the controls as the ship entered the atmosphere. Sweat dripped from his brows, and his hands shook. "Lower the landing gear," he told Luna.

Luna pressed a button. But as the landing gear came out, the heat from the reentry burned it up. The landing gear fell off, and the ship began to break up! "Our landing gear is toast!" Luna shouted.

Houston grabbed the phone. "Ham, you're going to crash—just like in the circus."

"Crash?" Luna asked, horrified.

"But this time, stay on target," Houston instructed.

Ham smiled. "Roger that, Houston."

Just then, Houston and Comet heard banging on the door. The guards were trying to get in!

"Come out with your thumbs up!" a guard shouted.

"Kick it down!" the senator ordered.

But as soon as they did, Houston and Comet zoomed out the door on their rocket packs.

The chimps flew past the guards, past the senator, past the scientists, and headed straight into a garage. They jumped into a huge rocket-mover truck and drove it onto the landing strip.

Houston pulled out a pair of binoculars and searched the sky. "No showboating," he said, when he spotted the ship in the air.

Inside the ship, Ham and Luna were struggling with the controls.

"I can't hold on!" Ham shouted as the ship shook violently.

Just then, the Zartog statue ripped off the front of the ship. The nose cone was useless!

The ship went into a spin.

"We lost steering control," Ham said.

Luna looked out the window and saw the rudder flapping. Thinking fast, she unbuckled her seat belt.

"What are you doing?" Ham asked.

"I'll see you on the ground," she said. And with that, she climbed onto the outside of the ship. She was going to fix the rudder!

Fighting the gravity forces, Luna struggled to wedge the rudder back into position. Finally, she did it, and the ship stabilized.

"Luna, you did it!" Ham shouted. He turned around to find her, but she was gone. "Luna!"

Ham knew he had to focus. The ground was coming up fast. Spotting the truck, he aligned the ship with his landing target.

Crash! The ship hit the target. But the impact sent the truck spinning down the landing strip. Sparks flew. Tires screeched. The truck skidded to a halt.

"Luna!" Ham cried, jumping out of the rocket and running to Luna's side. She was lying motionless on the ground nearby.

"Luna! Luna! Get up—you're okay, right?"

Ham leaned over Luna and cried. "I'm so sorry. I just wreck everything wherever I go. Just one crash after another. I should have been more like you. You were always . . ."

"Right?" Luna asked.

"Yes," Ham said with a whimper, too upset to see that Luna was okay. "And you made me . . ."

"Better," Luna finished.

"Yes. And if I had to be without you . . ."

"You won't be," Luna concluded. At that, Ham opened his eyes and saw Luna smiling up at him. He pulled her into a huge hug.

"But how did you survive?" Ham asked.

"Chin down, opposable thumbs in," she told him proudly.

Houston rushed over to Ham and patted him on the back. "Your grandpa was the first chimp in space, but you're the first chimp to save a planet."

The scientists couldn't believe their eyes. How

could the ship have made it back to Earth? Who could have reconstructed the ship? Was it the Space Chimps?

"They're political gold," the senator said, looking at the chimps.

"Senator, were you wrong to shut down the Space Agency?" a reporter asked.

"I-I-I," the senator stammered. Then, regaining his composure, he said, "I'd like to announce the opening of a high-tech space facility devoted to the exploration of deepest space."

Hearing this, the crowd went wild!

"Did the chimps encounter alien life?" a reporter asked the confused and awestruck scientists.

"Unfortunately, the onboard computer has been destroyed," Dr. Jagu reported. "So we will have to launch another mission to know for sure."

A few days later, the chimps got what they

wanted—a ticker tape parade! They sat on a giant float, waving to the crowds.

And the aliens on Planet Malgor got what they wanted, too—their planet was back to normal. All the statues were cracked, and the aliens were pulled out alive. And Kilowatt was the star of the Snizzlefruit Frolic Festival. She jumped up onstage and showed off the dance moves Ham had taught her. Gratefully, she looked up at the faces of Titan, Ham, and Luna that the aliens had carved into the side of the volcano. She would never forget her chimp friends.

And Zartog? Well, he got exactly what he deserved—he was a statue on the front lawn of a house in Florida. Oh, yeah—and he was the favorite place for the dog to pee!

THE END